Cabo San Lucas

A ROMANTIC COMEDY

by

Lisa Soland

SAMUEL FRENCH

FOUNDED 1830

NEW YORK HOLLYWOOD LONDON TORONTO

SAMUELFRENCH.COM

No one shall commit or authorize any act or omission by which the copyright of, or the right to copyright, this play may be impaired.

No one shall make any changes in this play for the purpose of production.

Publication of this play does not imply availability for performance. Both amateurs and professionals considering a production are strongly advised in their own interests to apply to Samuel French, Inc., for written permission before starting rehearsals, advertising, or booking a theatre.

No part of this book may be reproduced, stored in a retrieval system, or transmitted in any form, by any means, now known or yet to be invented, including mechanical, electronic, photocopying, recording, videotaping, or otherwise, without the prior written permission of the publisher.

IMPORTANT BILLING AND CREDIT REQUIREMENTS

All producers of *CABO SAN LUCAS must* give credit to the Author of the Play in all programs distributed in connection with performances of the Play, and in all instances in which the title of the Play appears for the purposes of advertising, publicizing or otherwise exploiting the Play and/or a production. The name of the Author *must* appear on a separate line on which no other name appears, immediately following the title and *must* appear in size of type not less than fifty percent of the size of the title type.

CABO SAN LUCAS was originally produced at The Tamarind Theatre in Hollywood, California, on November 2, 2002. It was directed by Linda L. Rand and produced by Sophie Rose Productions in association with The Florida Project. Lighting designer and stage manager was Joe Cabrera II. The cast, in order of appearance, was as follows:

JACK . . . . .Jeff Charlton

GUY. . . . . .Bill Lewis

GRACE. . . . . Lisa Soland

CAST OF CHARACTERS

JACK - 20's to 40's. The man in charge of robbing Grace. Impatient, quick to anger, and at times ominous and frightening.

GUY - 20's to 40's. The sweet, bumbling oaf who owns the gun that Jack needs to rob Grace. Happy-go-lucky, sweet and gentle.

GRACE - 20's to 40's. Sweet, honest and pure of heart. Prior to the start of the play, she's taken an overdose of sleeping pills.

SCENE

The living room of Grace's home in Los Angeles.

TIME

The middle of the night.

ABOUT THE AUTHOR

Lisa Soland's other Samuel French publications include her comedy *Waiting* and the romantic comedy *The Name Game*. *Waiting* can also be found in Smith & Kraus' anthology WOMEN PLAYWRIGHTS: THE BEST PLAYS OF 2003, and some of the monologues from *Cabo San Lucas* and *Waiting* are in BEST WOMEN'S STAGE MONOLOGUES OF 2003. Monologues from Ms. Soland's *The Rebirth, Red Roses* as well as *Waiting* are included in Applause Books' ONE ON ONE: THE BEST WOMEN'S MONOLOGUES FOR THE 21 ST CENTURY and ONE ON ONE: THE BEST MEN'S MONOLOGUES FOR THE 21 ST CENTURY. What has become known as "the straw scene" (Act I, Scene 2) in *Waiting*, is published in DUO: THE BEST SCENES FOR THE 21 ST CENTURY, also by Applause Books. Ms. Soland's other plays include *Truth Be Told, An Afternoon With Shirley, The Empty Chair, The Lord's Last Supper, Matt & His Crazy Writing Machine, Thread Count, Rebound and the Bathtub* and *The Christmas Tree Angel.*

Her ten-minute plays have received numerous productions and publications as well. *An Earthquake*, first directed by Charles Nelson Reilly, is included in Dramatic Publishing's anthology 35 IN 10, *Different* is part of Smith & Kraus' THE BEST TENMINUTE PLAYS OF 2005 (2 Actors), *The Same Thing* is in THE BEST TENMINUTE PLAYS OF 2006 (2 Actors), *Knots* is in THE BEST TEN-MINUTE PLAYS OF 2006 (3 Actors) and *The Other Shoe* in THE BEST TEN-MINUTE PLAYS OF 2008 (3 Actors).

Ms. Soland is a member of The Dramatists Guild of America, The Alliance of Los Angeles Playwrights and the International Centre for Women Playwrights. She founded one of Los Angeles' premiere playwright workshops - THE ALL ORIGINAL PLAYWRIGHT WORKSHOP – where she works as Artistic Director and teacher, helping to inspire countless new plays and productions.

*(SETTING: We are in **GRACE**'s stark living room. A large, tattered, old couch sits upstage center, away from the wall. Spread over the couch is a homemade, knitted blanket with two throw pillows on either end. In front of the couch is a coffee table with a large rug beneath it that extends out onto the floor.)*

(On the wall, upstage right, is a working window that opens and closes. Downstage right is the front door leading out, and upstage of that is another door that leads to the bedroom and kitchen. Upstage left is the doorway to the bathroom and a large, locked trunk sits downstage left. A second trunk is placed against the stage left wall, with a photo of Niagara Falls on it. Various boxes with names written on them are placed about the room.)

*(**AT RISE:** It is the middle of the night and the living room is pitch-dark. We hear some rattling near the keyhole on the offstage side of the front door. **JACK** and **GUY** enter carrying lit flashlights, each wearing a pair of two-legged pantyhose over their heads. **JACK** is the first to enter, with a handgun secured inside the front of his jeans, and two cloth laundry sacks tucked beneath his arm. Though they are both wearing black, it is clear who is who when the light of their flashlights is cast from one to another.)*

GUY. *(entering too close behind, he bumps into **JACK** in the dark)* Sorry!

JACK. *(turns quickly and shines the flashlight onto **GUY**'s face)* Shhh.

GUY. *(very quietly)* Sorry.

*(**JACK** crosses behind the couch while **GUY** moves upstage.)*

JACK. *(trips and falls)* Uggh!

GUY. *(quickly shining flashlight onto* **JACK***'s face)* Shhhhh!

JACK. *(pulling off the pantyhose)* I knew I was going to regret this.

> (**JACK** *gets up and the two men begin to rummage through the boxes as quietly as possible, which at this point…doesn't seem possible.)*

GUY. *(picks up a framed photograph, trying to whisper)* Oh, man. Look at this, Jack. Look at this photo. This must be the couple who lives here. Look at this. They're sitting by some nice, little…*(looking closer)*…fake waterfall. That's a fake waterfall!

JACK. Shhhh!

GUY. I hate fake waterfalls. They look so…fake.

JACK. Are you going to help me or not?

GUY. Ah, jeez. She's so pretty. And look at this jerk she's with. You can tell just by looking at him, he's no good. *(to self)* He's got his arms around her but he's no good.

JACK. Here. *(tosses one of his laundry sacks to* **GUY***)* Get stuffing.

GUY. *(looking at sack)* Oh, okay.

> (**GUY** *opens a box and quickly pulls something out to stuff into the sack, but it's a negligee.)*

Oh, man. Look at this.

> (**GUY** *tucks flashlight beneath his chin, which shines the light down onto the garment.)*

Look at this frilly thing. Jeez, I've never seen one of these up close before.

JACK. Never seen one up close? Where you been? A fucking cave?

GUY. Oh man, look at this – this netting thing that goes around the front. *(flipping it back to front)* Yeah, I guess that's the front, right?

JACK. *(shines the flashlight on what* **GUY** *is holding)* That's a negligee.

GUY. *(pronouncing out the word)* Negligee.

JACK. And white. Hmm. You don't see many white ones. Take it. We'll sell it on Ebay.

GUY. White. *(drops his flashlight which loudly hits the ground)* Oops.

JACK. Shhh!

(GRACE is lying on the couch, completely hidden beneath the blanket.)

GRACE. What's going on?

(GUY and JACK shine their flashlights onto the couch.)

GUY. I thought you said no one would be here.

(GRACE pokes her head out from beneath the blanket and shields her eyes from the light.)

GRACE. What are you doing?!

(JACK pulls out gun and directs it at GRACE.)

JACK. What are *you* doing?

GRACE. I live here. You better have just as good of an excuse.

GUY. Well, we don't live here.

GRACE. *(sitting up, confused)* Oh, I'm sorry.

GUY. It's not your fault.

GRACE. No, I mean the couch.

GUY. You're sorry for the couch?

JACK. Who could blame you?

GRACE. You're here for the couch, aren't you?

JACK. *(Using the flashlight, he looks at the couch.)* Uh, no. I think we'll leave that.

GRACE. *(suddenly angry, to JACK)* I waited for you till seven-thirty and you said you'd be back by five. That's just like me to wait. Well, I won't lie and tell you that someone else wanted it, but the least you could have done is called.

(To GUY)

Why didn't you call?

GUY. *(trying hard to come up with some excuse)* We…uh, didn't have your number.

GRACE. Didn't have my number?! Well, a considerate person would have stuck to their agreement and at least come by to say that they've changed their minds.

GUY. Well…uh…

GRACE. Oh, is that what you're here to tell me? You've changed your minds?

GUY. No! We, uhh…We felt we needed to see it again…in this light.

GRACE. Oh, is that all?

(With blanket wrapped around her, GRACE rises, crosses to light switch stage left, turns on light, then returns to couch.)

There.

(GUY removes the two-legged pantyhose to have a better look at the couch.)

GUY. Uh, yeah. We changed our minds. Let's go.

(He quickly turns to go.)

JACK. *(with gun pointed directly at GRACE)* Do you even see this gun in my hand?

GRACE. Yes, but its L.A. so I really didn't give it much thought.

JACK. Enough with the charades. We're not here for the couch. It's the middle of the night, for God's sake.

GUY. *(To GRACE)* You actually sold that couch?

GRACE. Fifteen dollars!

GUY. Fifteen dollars?

GRACE. *(She rises to display more of the couch.)* Yeah. Isn't that great?!

GUY. *(flatly telling the truth)* Yes.

JACK. *(To GUY)* Shut up.

(GRACE grows dizzy from rising so quickly.)

GRACE. Oh, my head.

(GRACE nearly bumps into the coffee table.)

GUY. Look out for the…

GRACE. *(sitting on couch)* Just before I went to sleep, I…

JACK. You are not supposed to be here.

GUY. You scared the heck out of us.

JACK. You were supposed to be on a plane…

GUY. *(finishing **JACK**'s sentence)* …bound for Cabo San Lucas.

GRACE. Oh yeah, yeah. *(beat)* Well, that didn't work out, I'm sorry to say.

(**JACK** *crosses to* **GUY** *and hands him the gun.*)

JACK. Here. You take the gun and keep it on her while I clean up.

GRACE. *(to **JACK**)* That's very nice of you. Thank you.

JACK. *(to **GUY**)* Sooner or later it's gonna hit her that she's being robbed…

GRACE. Robbed?

JACK. …and you'll need it. *(Takes **GUY**'s sack and turns to exit.)*

GRACE. *(It's starting to sink in.)* You gotta be kidding?!

JACK. *(turning back)* See? I told you.

(**JACK** *exits into bedroom/kitchen.*)

GRACE. You guys are robbing me?

GUY. *("sort of," holding the gun on **GRACE**)* Yeah. Well…sort of.

GRACE. Sort of? How can you "sort of" rob someone?

GUY. He's robbing you and I'm sort of just…

(**GRACE** *rises with blanket tucked around her and crosses to alarm box on wall near front door.*)

GRACE. I can't believe my alarm didn't go off.

GUY. You have an alarm?

GRACE. Oh, yeah.

GUY. Like a tiny, little, clock alarm on your nightstand sort-of-thing, to wake you up bright and cheery in the morning?

GRACE. No. Like a nice, huge, house-size deafening alarm clock that tells all the neighbors and a team of professionals that I'm being robbed.

GUY. Oh. *(beat)* There's no sign out front. You're supposed to have a sign.

GRACE. There was one – years ago, but it wore out. Like me.

(GRACE crosses to the window.)

GUY. Jeez, I wish we'd known that.

GRACE. That I wore out?

GUY. No, the alarm. Wish we'd known about the alarm.

GRACE. *(trying to open the window)* Yeah, I don't understand…

GUY. If we'd seen the sign, we wouldn't have…

GRACE. …I've never had a problem with it before.

GUY. You've been robbed before? Boy, that's karma for you. Here, let me help you with that.

(GUY crosses to the window and without thinking, tries to help GRACE open it.)

GRACE. No, no. It just goes off every time I come home.

GUY. Do you have it set up that way?

(GUY can't open the window either.)

GRACE. *(sitting on right arm of couch)* No, it's just me. I set it off by accident and it's awful 'cause I…

(Something's wrong with her tongue.)

Yuck.

(GRACE uses a piece of her blanket to wipe off her tongue.)

Something's wrong with my tongue. *(beat)* I'm sorry. What was I saying?

GUY. No, that's okay. Uh…"tripping it by accident…"

(GRACE still looks confused. GUY tries to help her remember.)

The alarm.

GRACE. *(rising and crossing to box of tissue on trunk, downstage left)* Oh, yeah, accident. The whole thing was a stupid accident. And it's awful 'cause I never remember the code.

GUY. Bummer.

GRACE. What time is it?

GUY. Time for you to get a new alarm.

GRACE. *(wiping off tongue with tissue)* No, time. The time?

GUY. *(looking at watch)* Three thirty-three.

GRACE. *(deep in thought)* Wow. Three thirty-three. *(beat)* How long you guys been in here?

GUY. The code. You were saying something about the code.

GRACE. Oh, yeah. Well, you know, they call on the phone usually within the first three minutes of a break-in and they ask you the code and I usually just stand there thinking, "What the heck is my freakin' code?!"

GUY. "Freakin'." I thought I was the only one whoever said that.

GRACE. "Freakin'?"

GUY. Yeah.

GRACE. Oh, yeah.

GUY. Why do you say it?

GRACE. To avoid saying…

GUY. *(finishing her sentence)* …the "f" word?

GRACE. Yes.

GUY. Me too. It's such a harsh word.

GRACE. Very harsh.

(**GRACE** *crosses to the bathroom.*)

GUY. *(holding gun up to* **GRACE***)* Hey, where you going?

GRACE. If you guys are going to be here a while, I'm going to need some aspirin.

GUY. Oh, no, you have to stay here. I'll get them for you.

(**GUY** *begins to cross to bathroom. Suddenly* **GRACE** *guards the door.*)

GRACE. No! No. You can't go in there.

GUY. You'll let me rob you but I can't go in your bathroom?

GRACE. No, no, please!

(**GUY** *stops to listen.*)

GRACE. (*trying to come up with some excuse*) I just started my… uh…you know – the once-a-month, thing.

GUY. (*too much information*) Oh, right, right.

(*He quickly turns downstage.*)

GRACE. I'll get them. Can I? Please?

GUY. (*notices some sort of sleeping pad on the couch*) Hey. What's this?

GRACE. Oh, nothing.

GUY. I think I've seen these advertised on infomercials or something.

GRACE. Listen, can I get the aspirin or not?

GUY. (*preoccupied*) Yeah, yeah. Sure, sure.

(**GRACE** *exits to bathroom.*)

GUY. (*lifting pad, syudying it*) What does it do? Vibrate?

GRACE. (*offstage*) Vibrate?

GUY. Yeah.

GRACE. (*offstage*) God, no. My fiancé…ex-fiancé…would have loved that. (*re-entering briefly, with bottle of aspirin*) It just lies there while you lay on it. (*pops two in her mouth*) Like him.

GUY. (*placing pad back on the couch*) Jeez, I'm really sorry about that.

GRACE. And *I* was the one with the problem.

(**GRACE** *exits into bathroom again.*)

GUY. So…what is it?

GRACE. (*offstage*) A magnetic pad.

GUY. Oh. And you sleep on it?

GRACE. You get the maximum effect that way.

(**GUY** *crawls over the back of the couch and lies down on pad in fetal position, trying to fit his entire body onto the pad.*)

GUY. Tiny, little thing. Isn't it?

GRACE. *(entering)* Well, I couldn't afford the whole mattress pad. This is the car seat pad. I just curl up little and tiny when I sleep and I saved close to eight hundred dollars.

GUY. So what does it do?

GRACE. *(sitting on left arm of couch)* I'm not sure. My fiancé… *(hits herself in the head, correcting herself)*…ex-fiancé, said I had a problem with my…sex drive, and it's supposed to help with your circulation…

(**GUY** *quickly jumps off pad and sits on the right arm of the couch.*)

…but I don't think it worked. You probably think that's crazy, don't you?

GUY. Well, no. It makes sense. *(plainly)* It didn't work.

GRACE. No. But it did get rid of my carpal tunnel. But he didn't care about my carpal tunnel.

GUY. Oh, that's great.

GRACE. No, it's not.

GUY. I mean the fact that it went away – the tunnel.

GRACE. Oh, yeah, well it doesn't matter now.

(**GRACE** *rises and crosses behind couch to bedroom/ kitchen door.*)

What's your friend doing in there?

GUY. *(rising)* He's cleaning you out.

GRACE. Oh.

(**GRACE** *looks at bedroom/kitchen door, then back to* **GUY.**)

You don't mean vacuuming, do you, because I hate vacuuming and I was kind of hoping…?

(**GUY** *shakes his head.* **GRACE** *looks back to bedroom/ kitchen door and after just a moment's thought…*)

GRACE. Okay. *(beat)* Do you mind if I go back to sleep now?

GUY. *(surprised at her lax attitude)* No. No. That's fine, I guess. Go ahead and lie down.

GRACE. *(sits on couch)* I'm really tired.

GUY. *(observing her)* You look really tired. And what were you doing here, by the way? You were supposed to be in Cabo San Lucas.

GRACE. *(cringing)* Oh, don't say that. I hate that freakin' place. I hate hearing about it. *(fluffing couch pillows with fervor)* That's all he ever said, "Cabo San Lucas! Cabo San Lucas!" – like it was the only good thing that was ever going to happen to us. *(beat)* You know you're in trouble when the only good thing that happens to you during your marriage, is your honeymoon.

GUY. Yeah. I suppose it should just get better from there, not worse.

GRACE. *(trying to lie down to sleep)* Although they do say, "For better and for worse."

GUY. Yes, but you shouldn't plan for the worse. Hard things happen in life…

(GRACE discovers GUY's gun lying on the couch and using only two fingers, lifts it up for GUY to take from her. Embarrassed, he takes gun and holds it on her again.)

Well, hard things should be expected, but not planned for. That's all I'm saying.

GRACE. *(waking up a bit)* Hey, wait a second. How come you knew I was…? I don't even know you. Do I?

GUY. *(nervously, crossing behind couch, trying to explain)* We've been tracking your mail. Actually, Jack was…*(trying to quickly cover)* I mean, John. That guy in there – John, John.

GRACE. "John, John." Funny name.

GUY. He's a funny guy.

GRACE. His name is Jack. It's no big deal. You don't have

to lie to me.

GUY. *(completely relieved)* Oh, thank you. *(sitting on the left arm of couch)* You're right – "Jack." And I hate lying, by the way.

GRACE. You hate lying but you can rob a house or two.

GUY. Well, no. Things aren't always as they first seem. You see he…Jack, kind of tricked me into… He didn't have a gun, you see, and…

GRACE. *(interrupting)* Oh, it's your gun.

GUY. *(rising)* Yes. Yes it is. My Dad's gun, actually. It was the only thing he left me so I…*(beat)* Can I finish?

GRACE. I'm sorry, go on.

(Wanting to finish with his confession, GUY crosses behind couch.)

GUY. Jack found your airline tickets in the mail and steamed them open to find out when you weren't going to be here and then planned to do all of this while you were gone.

(GRACE picks up envelope/airline tickets from the coffee table and looks at them.)

He hates confrontation. It makes him nervous. That's why he gets so angry. You should have seen him asking me for the gun.

GRACE. *(joking)* What is he, a postman or something?

GUY. Actually yes, I'm sorry to say.

GRACE. Jeez.

GUY. I couldn't believe it either 'cause, well, you know. *(sitting on small table stage right)* You want to believe in those guys – those "Come rain or come shine" guys. Only sometimes it ain't true. Sometimes it's, "Come rain and come some more rain."

GRACE. I know about rain. Go on.

GUY. I mean, just 'cause they got the uniforms doesn't mean they're a bundle of sunshine. You gotta judge 'em each separately, just like everybody else.

GRACE. *(placing airline tickets back on coffee table)* I guess that's really using your noggin' though, you know? Looking at airline tickets sent through the mail.

GUY. Yeah, but of all places to use your "noggin"!

GRACE. If you don't approve, why are you here?

GUY. Well, I was simply telling Jack the story of my overbearing father and how he left me this gun and how much Jack reminds me of him…and the next thing I know, Jack's got the gun to my head and he's telling me *his* story – his plan on how to rob you.

GRACE. *His* plan.

GUY. Yeah, the plot.

GRACE. The plot?

GUY. Yeah. And considering the fact that he's got a gun to my head, and it's my gun, I thought I better just come along and see how his story played itself out.

GRACE. *(becoming more and more tired)* You must be a writer.

GUY. No, no unfortunately. A writer is someone who actually writes. So, no. That wouldn't be me. I *think* about writing. All day long. Just *think* about it. Like I *think* about doing everything else. But that doesn't make me a writer.

GRACE. Nope, but it does make you a robber because you are actually robbing me.

GUY. *(with realization)* Yes. I'm afraid you're right.

GRACE. Yup, that's the problem. If you don't do something about *your* story, someone comes along and makes you do something about *theirs*. And then you end up not liking the ending and there's nothing you can do about it because it's too late.

GUY. Yeah, maybe.

GRACE. It's too late.

GUY. Maybe you're right.

(**GRACE** *rises and crosses to alarm box on the wall downstage right.*)

GRACE. I wonder why the alarm didn't go off.

GUY. Fortunate, I guess. For us, I mean.

(*JACK enters with goods from bedroom/kitchen, along with both sacks, which are now full.*)

JACK. Okay, it's all out.

(*JACK notices that* GUY *does not have the gun pointed at* GRACE. GUY *quickly raises his arm with gun, and points it at her.*)

Tie her up, please. (*Throwing rope to* GUY *with disgust*) Do you think you can manage that? A simple knot?

GUY. Yes, I think I can knot.

(*JACK physically intimidates* GRACE *away from the front door and back into the room.*)

JACK. I'll move all this to the back door and then I'll go get the car.

(*He exits with the goods.* GRACE *and* GUY *stand awkwardly looking at each other.*)

GRACE. Well, I guess that's that. End of story.

GUY. Yeah. (*gesturing to rope*) Gee, do you mind?

GRACE. Oh no, here. (*offering* GUY *her wrists*) Can you do them in front, in case I get an itch?

GUY. Sure, you kidding?!

(*He begins to tie* GRACE's *wrists together in the front.*)

Listen, I'm sorry about the uh…

GRACE. (*a little too casually*) Oh, no. It's okay. (*beat*) I sold everything anyway, in the pre-honeymoon garage sale.

GUY. (*finally putting it all together*) You were going on your honeymoon?

GRACE. Yeah. Well, not now. It doesn't matter. The stuff that I kept, I was going to leave for my family. You know, the valuable stuff I thought they would want, but I don't care. You can have it. (*beat*) Did you get the silver?

GUY. Oh, I don't know. Hold on, I'll ask. (*yelling out the closed window*) Jack, did you get the…? (*trying to open the window*) Jack! (*beginning to bang on the window glass*) Did you get…?!

*(Hitting a deeper level of "tired," **GRACE** crosses to couch and sits. **JACK** enters quickly. He pulls **GUY** forcibly away from window.)*

GUY. Hey, hey, hey, hey, hey! When you're in the middle of a robbery, you don't yell.

GUY. *(losing a bit of his patience)* Well, thank you. I'm really so glad to have such a good, hands-on instructor through all of this. Can I talk now? Is it okay if I talk?

JACK. What?

GUY. She wanted to know if we got the silver.

JACK. Silver? *(turning and moving toward **GRACE**)* No, no I did not get the silver. *(To **GRACE**)* Should I have?

GRACE. Oh, yeah. It's valuable and he left it. He forgot it, actually. I was questioning whether or not to send it to him because he owed me a lot of money as it was.

GUY. *(in disbelief)* Man, who is this jerk?

JACK. Quiet!!! *(To **GRACE**, very focused)* Where is it?

GRACE. Sorry. I get off track when I'm talking about my fiancé…*(knocking herself in the head again)*…ex-fiancé, 'cause I'm pretty much still processing what happened.

JACK. Get it.

*(**GRACE** retrieves a key that is hidden in the arm of the couch.)*

GUY. Oh, here. *(hands gun to **JACK**)*

JACK. *(To **GUY**)* You keep it. You're doing fine.

GUY. No, I really don't want it any more. Thanks, though.

*(**GUY** tries to hand **JACK** the gun and **JACK** slams the gun back into his stomach.)*

GUY. *(continued)* Oh. Okay.

GRACE. *(seeing **GUY** is getting hurt, timidly to **JACK**)* Do you want me to get it for you?

GUY. *(quickly trying to protect her)* No. You stay in bed. Couch. I mean couch. You stay there.

GRACE. *(holding up key)* I have the key.

JACK. Then get it!

(GRACE *quickly rises and the blanket falls down from around her, revealing a nicely shaped body in a soft nightgown. She takes a step toward the trunk and trips over the blanket, then falls to the ground.* JACK *notices her shapely figure and the energy in the room suddenly changes.*)

GUY. *(stooping to help her with the blanket)* Here. You dropped…

(*Putting his arm out,* JACK *stops* GUY *from helping her.*)

JACK. No. Let *her.*

(GRACE *slowly sits up from the fall and becomes dizzy. She takes a breath and then tries to open the trunk.*)

GUY. *(crossing to* GRACE*)* Here, let me help you with that.

GRACE. That's very kind of you.

(GUY *sits beside her and takes the key. He opens the trunk and lifts out an elaborate set of silver in a beautiful, velvet container.*)

GRACE. *(to* GUY, *happy to contribute)* It was our wedding present from his mother. It's like, real silver.

JACK. Is it "like" real silver or is it real silver?

GRACE. *(to* JACK*)* Oh no, it's like the real thing.

JACK. *(pressing the issue)* Is it "like" the real thing or is it…?

(*Losing more of his patience,* GUY *rises to show* JACK.*)

GUY. Jack! It's real. It's real! Look! Can't you tell the real thing when you see it?!

JACK. *(with eyes fixated on* GRACE*)* Yes, I sure can.

GRACE. *(to* JACK*)* You'll do good with that, trust me.

(GRACE *begins to hit yet a deeper level of incognizance.*)

JACK. Okay, I think I will.

(JACK *crosses to* GUY *and hands him car keys. He then quickly escorts him to the front door.*)

Here. Go get the car. And take your time. Pull around the side, through the alley and wait for me there.

GUY. *(sensing trouble)* Oh. Are you sure? I mean, I don't drive very well and...

JACK. Give me the gun.

GUY. What, this gun?

JACK. Yes, this gun.

GUY. How 'bout I take it with me? She's really nice and has been quite helpful, really. You probably won't need it for the very short time I'm gone.

JACK. *(takes gun from* **GUY***)* Go!

GUY. *(backing out of the room)* Oh, okay.

JACK. Now!

> *(**JACK** points gun at **GUY** to get rid of him faster.)*

GUY. Right. Right.*(beginning to exit)* But if you should need anything, I'll be right out... Well, around the corner and up the block...walking. Parking in this town! It's such a hassle.

> *(**GUY** exits with the silver. **JACK** turns back into the room, menacingly)*

JACK. I'm sorry, Miss. I missed your name. And I should know your name. *(crossing toward her, slowly)* I mean, anyone who looks this nice in the middle of a cold, dark night, deserves to have her name known and known well. And...

> *(**JACK** checks to make certain they are alone.)*

I want to know you...uh...

> *(He puts the gun into his pocket and kneels beside* **GRACE.***)*

GRACE. *(trying to keep her eyes open)* Grace.

JACK. Grace.

> *(**JACK** begins to touch her sensuously.)*

I want to know you very well, Grace, for at least one, brief moment before I leave.

GRACE. *(barely awake)* I know you're talking. I can hear you talking...but I'm... If you wouldn't mind me just catching a few winks and then I'll just…wink away.

*(From her sitting position, **GRACE** finally collapses onto the trunk, completely exhausted. **JACK**'s ego is wounded and the anger comes.)*

JACK. Yes, actually, I would mind you winking. Get up.

(She doesn't move.)

I said, get up!!! *(forcibly yanking **GRACE** to her feet)* He tied your arms in the front. Why?

GRACE. In case I got an itch. It's my fault. I asked him to.

*(**JACK** drags **GRACE** to the couch and sets her down on the left arm.)*

JACK. Well, I got an itch too. And I'm going to itch it just the way I like.

*(**JACK** angrily unties **GRACE**'s hands.)*

GRACE. Ouch!

*(Once untied, **JACK** goes to undo his pants, which leaves **GRACE** unsteadily balanced on the couch's arm. She leans forward into **JACK** then falls back onto the sofa, dead asleep. She lets out a big, fat, ugly snore. The window opens, upstage right, and an arm pokes its way through, waving up and down. This movement sets off the house alarm.)*

JACK. Holy ever-lovin' fuck!!!

(He runs to the window.)

GRACE. My, that's loud.

JACK. *(hands over his ears, trying to redo pants)* Turn it off! Can't you turn it off?!

*(He crosses to **GRACE**.)*

Get up.

(He shakes her.)

Wake up. What the hell's wrong with you?!

*(He shakes her forcibly. **GUY** enters and boldly pulls **JACK** off **GRACE**.)*

GUY. You got your stuff, now get out of here.

JACK. The alarm, you idiot. We won't get far now. Wake her up. She's going to have to answer the phone when they call. And they always call.

(*JACK crosses to open door downstage right, quickly looks out, then closes it.*)

They ask for some secret…(*trying hard to remember the word*) …thing-a-ma-jig and she's got to give it to them or we're fried.

GUY. Code.

JACK. What?

GUY. Code. The word you were looking for is "code."

JACK. (*Not to be corrected, he angrily crosses back to couch.*) Get her up.

GUY. She's tired, Jack. Let her sleep.

JACK. Stand her up!

GUY. If she ain't wakin' up with that, I say she ain't wakin' up.

(*JACK grabs GRACE and tries to make her stand.*)

Hey! Be careful. She's not unbreakable, you know.

(*The very loud alarm continues to sound throughout as JACK tries to wake GRACE. She is limp in his arms.*)

She must have gotten drunk or something. She's been out of it all night.

JACK. Get some water.

(*GUY exits to bathroom.*)

JACK. (*continued*) (*standing GRACE up*) Where's your phone, sweetheart? Let's get you over…

(*He drags her around the room looking for phone.*)

… to the phone. (*To self*) Wherever the fuck it is.

GRACE. (*suddenly talking*) Peaceful…

JACK. (*with hope*) Is that the code – "peaceful?" Is that it?

GRACE. (*continuing to ramble*) I imagined this would be a peaceful, loving, gentle thing.

JACK. What?

GUY. *(offstage)* Oh my God!

JACK. What now?!

GUY. *(entering with water, prescription pills and whiskey bottle)* Oh my God. Jack, I can't believe it!

JACK. *(to GUY)* What, no water?

GUY. No, here – water.

> (**JACK** *takes water and throws it on* **GRACE***'s face, which opens her eyes, momentarily. She falls back onto the coffee table.*)

Look at this. She's gone and taken sleeping pills.

GRACE. Sleeping pills!

GUY. She's taken sleeping pills.

GRACE. Sleeping pills!!

> (**JACK** *begins to slap* **GRACE***'s face to wake her.*)

JACK. I heard you the first time.

GUY. Sleeping pills, Jack.

GRACE. Sleeping pills, Jack!

JACK. Yes. It's common, you know. People do take them.

GUY. Yes, in two's and three's, because they're having trouble sleeping, but not the entire prescription in one night. *(lifting up the bottle of whiskey)* With whiskey.

> (**JACK** *continues to slap* **GRACE***'s face*)

JACK. Yes. Believe me, my mother used to do it all the time.

GUY. No, no. You're not getting it. She's… Oh God. It's all making sense now. I mean we're robbing her, for God's sake.

JACK. Well, not for God's sake. For mine.

> (**JACK** *gives up on* **GRACE** *and crosses to couch, pulling it apart looking for the phone.* **GRACE** *begins to lie down and just before her head hits the coffee table,* **GUY** *places a pillow beneath it.*)

GUY. We're robbing her and she's just letting us! *(looking over the place and putting it all together)* She's sold all of her things and leaving the rest to her family. Look at this! She's got the stuff in boxes with their names on them and now she's letting us take all of that without fighting because she doesn't care. She's trying to kill herself!

JACK. *(searching through the boxes for phone)* Just my fucking luck.

GUY. She's trying to end the one, perfect thing we're given.

JACK. What are you, a poet?

GUY. I wish.

JACK. Find the phone, Shakespeare, before it rings.

GUY. *(Standing right beside the phone, he picks it up.)* It's right here.

JACK. Oh, good.

(He crosses to **GRACE** *and lifts her up from the coffee table.)*

Now get some more water. We need her conscious when they call.

GUY. We need more than that. We need an ambulance.

*(***GUY*** starts to dial 9-1-1.* **JACK** *drags* **GRACE** *to the couch and tosses her there, just in time to hang up phone and take it from* **GUY***.)*

JACK. Don't even tell me you were about to dial nine, one, one. Don't even tell me that. Because I don't want to know how truly stupid you are. *(suddenly loud)* Are you fucking kidding me? Nine, one, one? Oh, that's great. Let's just call the fucking cops and tell them where we are and what we've been up to so they can throw my ass in jail once again but this time for *armed* robbery. That's just great. Oh, and let's not forget to tell them that we're holding a hostage. *(crossing behind couch)* We're holding a hostage when she's supposed to be in CABO SAN LUCAS!!!

GRACE. *(reacting to "Cabo" with a high-pitched screech)* Uhhhh!

*(***GUY*** crosses to* **GRACE***.* **JACK** *grabs* **GUY** *and throws*

him to the ground, holding the gun to his head.)

GUY. Hey, be careful. My dad gave me that gun.

JACK. And he's dead, so now you gotta listen to *me*, fuck head. *(beat)* We're gonna get her ready for that phone call and then we're gonna get the hell out of here. Got it?

GUY. Okay, sure.

(With difficulty, GRACE *sits up on couch.)*

GRACE. I was going to be like Anne Bancroft in that Sidney Poitier movie…

JACK. *(to* GRACE*)* Shut up!

GRACE. *(continuing, to no one in particular)* …where she takes the pills, those peaceful, little pills.

JACK. *(back to* GUY*, with sarcasm)* But first we have to figure out how to shut off that fucking alarm before the whole city drops by for tea.

GRACE. *(manages to stand and make her way to the alarm box)* I mean, if I wanted this, if I wanted violence and abuse, I would have just shot myself in the head.

(She punches in some numbers and the alarm shuts off. She takes a few steps back into the room and then gracefully collapses to the floor. The phone rings. JACK *jumps up and* GUY *quickly follows.)*

(loudly) Hello. Where am I?

(Silence. Both men stand frozen, staring at each other. GUY *crosses to* GRACE *and kneels beside her, making sure she's all right.)*

JACK. The phone is ringing and you need to answer it.

*(*JACK *quickly gets the phone and kneels on the other side of* GRACE.*)*

That's what we do when phones ring.

(He lifts GRACE *up to a sitting position so she can talk.)*

It's the alarm people and they're calling for your…

GUY. Code.

JACK. Code. The code. Hey loser, do you remember your fucking code?

(*He puts phone into* GRACE*'s hand.*)

GUY. (*gently, to* GRACE) It would be ever so helpful.

GRACE. (*to* GUY) It would be ever so helpful if he'd stop using the "f" word.

GUY. (*to* JACK, *as mediator*) She would respond better if you treated her gentler, Jack. She's one of the gentler kind.

(GRACE *presses the "talk" button, but is holding the phone out in front of her.*)

GRACE. Hello. How are you people doing?

(JACK *moves phone to her ear.*)

Pardon? Oh, good. That's very good. (*beat*) Well, it's late or early, certainly in the middle of the night and one might think at such a time as this, that this was the real McCoy, that I was actually being robbed or raped or a little of both, wouldn't one?

(JACK *jabs gun into* GRACE*'s side, as* JACK *and* GUY. *stand her up in order to keep her awake.*)

But...lo and behold, I am not. I'm not. Really. In fact, I think I just opened the window...or not.

(GRACE *starts to fall asleep, standing, so* GUY *and* JACK *begin to walk her around the living room.*)

You know what it is? It's the spiders. They build their webs in the upper corners of the room, across the little beam of light and eventually it just cuts it off – the light. No more light.

(*She droops forward.* GUY *and* JACK *lift* GRACE *back up.*)

At least that's what the man told me after he came out the last time I set it off. He said...

JACK. (*Pressing gun deeper into* GRACE*'s ribs, he whispers into her ear.*) Tell her the fucking code.

GRACE. *(still into phone)* Excuse me, what is your name? *(To* **JACK**, *correctively)* It's a "him" not a "her."

JACK. Tell *him.*

GRACE. Listen, Brian… I'm in a bit of a jam here. Last night I took some sleeping pills so I'm a little in-cog-ni-sito.

JACK. *(forcefully, pushing the gun into* **GRACE***'s ribs)* The code.

GRACE. Oh, yeah. *(beat)* The code is… *(beat)* What the heck is my freakin' code?

> *(Having to think deeply,* **GRACE** *falls asleep again.* **GUY** *and* **JACK** *begin to walk her around the back of the couch and as they do, she climbs up and onto the back of the couch to lie down.)*

Gosh, it's a difficult world we live in, isn't it? So many codes to remember – E-trade, A.O.L., A.T.M., Visa, debit or credit…*(suddenly remembering)* Oh. I got it. It's the uh…

> *(***GRACE** *gets up, on her own, and crosses downstage.* **GUY** *and* **JACK** *follow.)*

It's the uh…name of the girl who loses her petals.

JACK. *(trying to guess)* Linda Lovelace.

GRACE. *(Looking at* **JACK** *in disgust, she crosses away.)* Brian, you sound like a hu-man-i-narian-type person. It's the dear little girl – the daughter of Jimmy Stewart – her name. She loses the petals to her flower that the teacher gave her in school that day.

GUY. *(It's becoming a game show.)* It's A Wonderful Life!

> *(He covers his own mouth, afraid of being heard over the phone.)*

GRACE. *(looking at* **GUY***)* Yes!

GUY. It's my favorite movie. *(covering his own mouth again)*

GRACE. *(To* **GUY***)* Oh my God, me too. My God, that is so sweet.

GUY. Zu Zu. *(quickly covers own mouth)*

GRACE. *(back to phone)* "Zu Zu's Petals" is the code. You're welcome. *(to* **GUY***)* Thank you. *(into phone)* Pardon?

*(Afraid she will say something wrong, **JACK** presses gun into **GRACE**'s ribs.)*

No, no. I'm fine. No, no ambulance. I'm just gonna lie back down here and…*(beat)* No, just two. Two little pills, the usual amount.

*(**GRACE** collapses and **GUY** catches her, mid-fall, and lowers her to the floor. **GUY** hangs up the phone and places it beside her.)*

GUY. Some "usual amount."

JACK. *(turning to **GUY**, with hand outstretched)* Give me the keys.

GUY. What, these keys? *(taking them from pocket)*

JACK. Yes, "these keys."

*(**JACK** moves menacingly toward **GUY**, who backs up around the couch.)*

GUY. Okay, but before I give them to you, I want you to tell me one thing. What makes somebody like you, cause all this trouble?

JACK. I can't live on what the government pays me!

GUY. *(sitting on right arm of couch, passionately trying to help)* Oh, Jack. Yes you can! You just have to learn to budget.

*(**JACK** points gun at **GUY**'s chest.)*

GUY. *(trying to explain)* We all have to live on what we make, Jack.

JACK. I don't have to do jack shit, fuck head.

*(**JACK** takes the keys from **GUY**.)*

I'm out of here. *(beat)* And next time I need a gun…

GUY. *(cutting him off, parentally)* You'll buy your own.

*(**JACK** hits **GUY** on the back of the head with the heal of the pistol.)*

Oh, God.

*(**GUY** falls to the ground in front of the couch, next to **GRACE**. **JACK** wipes his fingerprints from the gun and tosses it onto sofa.)*

JACK. Like they're gonna sell a gun to a postal employee.

(JACK *exits. The room grows silent.*)

GUY. My father may be dead but he keeps getting me into trouble. *(beat)* Come on, Guy. No time to be knocked out cold. You can't let the story end like this, for God's sake. You have to wake up. You have to do something. *(beat)* I am awake and choosing to not be knocked out cold. *(thinking to himself)* Can a person do that? Can a person choose their own ending? Okay. I must not be knocked out or I wouldn't be able to talk to myself. Now, think, Guy. Think. What do you do for someone with an overdose? What does one do? Coffee! I'll get some coffee in her, if I could just…wake up. I need to call the…uh… Wait!

(*He quickly sits up, then feels the throbbing on his head where he was hit with the gun.*)

Owww. What if I call? Who am I? What am I doing here? The place is empty, but for a five dollar couch…

GRACE. *(moaning)* Fifteen.

GUY. *(reaching for tickets on coffee table)* …and two tickets to Cabo San Lucas.

GRACE. *(the high pitched moan)* Uhhhhhh.

GUY. Sorry.

(**GUY** *crawls to* **GRACE.**)

Why did you do this? Could you tell me that? Is it 'cause of this one guy, this…fake waterfall fellow? Because nobody's worth this. No one.

(**GUY** *turns* **GRACE** *toward him and looks into her face.*)

GRACE. No.

GUY. Why then? What could have been so bad? You're so pretty. You've got your whole…*(beat)* …everything going for you.

(*With great sadness,* **GRACE** *turns away from* **GUY.**)

What? Why?

(GUY pulls GRACE into a sitting position and leans her against coffee table.)

Even me, who has no backbone whatsoever, who changes himself depending on who is around him, like some big ol' lump of tofu. Even me – "Tofu Genius of the Century." Even I understand the gift of life.

(GUY sits beside GRACE.)

GRACE. What's your name?

GUY. Guy.

GRACE. No, it's okay. You can tell me. I'm… Well, I like you anyway. I'm not going to tell anyone what's gone on here.

GUY. Guy. My name is Guy.

GRACE. Guy? Who named you that?

GUY. You know – the people who do the naming.

GRACE. It's a lovely name.

GUY. Tell me, why are you through with this living thing?

GRACE. I'm tired.

GUY. Yes, I know. The pills.

GRACE. *(beginnning to slip from sitting position)* No, no. I'm tired, tired. Of everything.

(GUY picks her back up.)

Taking a shower, brushing my teeth, eating. Facing the day. Everyday things. I'm so freakin' tired of them. They do nothing but remind me that I'm by myself.

GUY. Alone.

GRACE. Yeah.

(GRACE slips again and GUY picks her up on her feet and moves her to the couch.)

I mean, I've been alone my whole…pretty much, my life. But it got harder as I got older. I watched all my friends get married and have children and their lives just get so busy. Have you no idea how busy everyone is?

(GUY exits to bathroom.)

So busy? The whole world. Buzzing, buzzing, buzzing. And they have to let you know how busy they are. *(Calling out to GUY)* Have you ever noticed that? They have to let you know how busy they are so it really sinks in how truly insignificant you are to them and it's just because you've set different priorities than them. That's all.

(GUY re-enters with a wet washcloth and lays it across GRACE's forehead.)

Priorities like sitting and talking and listening and doing nothing...nothing but being with each other.

(GUY exits through bedroom/kitchen door.)

But heck, your priorities don't matter because there's no one really to do *your* priorities with, but yourself, because everyone else is so...buzzing.

(GUY re-enters with bowl of ice.)

No one really sees each other any more.

GUY. *(trying to understand)* Sees? I don't understand.

(With washcloth, he applies ice water to GRACE's face and neck.)

GRACE. *(pushing it away)* Ah!

GUY. Sorry.

(He slowly reapplies the washcloth.)

GRACE. No one really sees you! No one even really looks. No one has time to look. And even if they do? Even if by some strange accident, yours and another person's eyes meet in this busy world... they still don't really see you. Take you in. Not really. *(looking out)* I see *them*. I see them and I see the pain. And I see them not being able to see me.

GUY. Too busy.

GRACE. *(Very vulnerable, she nods.)* It's like I'm not even here. Though I feel so...here. It gets confusing.

GUY. *(carefully places his hand on* **GRACE***'s hand)* I see you, Grace.

(They have a moment like **GRACE** *has just described.* **GUY** *really "sees" her and she feels it.)*

GRACE. How do you know my name?

GUY. The airline tickets to Cabo…

GRACE. *(a high-pitched plea)* Don't say it!

GUY. Sorry. Where did *you* want to go on your…?

(He stops himself from saying a potentially upsetting word.)

GRACE. Honeymoon?

GUY. Yeah.

GRACE. *(referring to picture leaning against stage left trunk)* Niagara Falls.

GUY. *(Rising, He crosses to picture and picks it up.)* Oh, gee. I've always wanted to go there – Niagara Falls. Always.

(He crosses back to **GRACE***.)*

Ever since I was a kid.

GRACE. *(growing deeper in her sorrow)* He said it's trashed now. It's not like it used to be in the fifties, when people married for life. "For life."

(Stumbling, she makes her way to photo of her with ex-fiancé and the fake waterfall.)

That's what he said, "For Life," and it ended between the proposal and the marriage vows. Some life. Could you ever do such a thing to a person?!

GUY. No.

GRACE. *(She sits on small, stage right table, to steady herself.)* People ask about it, why it ended, and I don't know what to say to them? How to explain?

GUY. Yes, but at least they ask, Grace.

GRACE. *(becoming upset)* Yes, but they don't hear my answer. They don't hear what I say to them. They only hear what would have happened if it was happening to them, in their life. But not to me. Not me in my life.

Their life. You see?

(She stands with photo and looks into it as if it were a mirror.)

I'm just a reflection of them in their lives. I don't exist. They don't hear me, Guy, and I don't exist.

*(So full of pain and sleeping pills, **GRACE** stumbles forward. **GUY** catches her and lowers her onto the couch.)*

GUY. Grace, my dear Grace. I want so much to hear all about everything you have to say, but I have to do something, here. Right now. I need to make a decision about what to do and actually *do* something, for a change. *(beat)* Let me make you some coffee. Can I?

*(**GRACE** shakes her head.)*

I'll call for an ambulance… Or you… Are you okay enough to… Can I…? It would be better if I drove you in. Then they wouldn't… *(beat)* Actually…I have no car! My car is back at… Jack, he's uh…*(taking a breath)* Here. I'm going to call.

(He crosses to phone, downstage left.)

I'm just going to make the call.

*(He starts to dial the phone. **GRACE** finds the gun in the couch and points it at **GUY**, almost steady.)*

GRACE. Put down the phone. You're not calling anyone. You've got your whole life in front of you. Those were the words you were trying to say to me earlier but you couldn't, but it's true for you, Guy. You really do. *(beat)* And it's obvious you have no criminal experience prior to this evening…so I'm not going to let you throw away your future just because I have none. I've made my choice.

GUY. Yes, but you know suicide, what they say – "It's a permanent solution to a…"

*(**GRACE** crosses to left arm of couch and sits. Her words are beginning to really slur.)*

GRACE. "…to a temporary problem." Yes, I know but that's where they're wrong. My problem is not a temporary one, you see? This has been going on for a very long time. I have always felt alone, my entire life. If the world was different somehow, slower maybe… Jeez, I don't know. *(finding the right words, with strength)* If people could see someone who isn't like them. *(beat)* Well, anyway, that's why I can do this. I'm an exception.

GUY. God doesn't look favorably at such things. At exceptions.

(GRACE moves closer to him and sits on the coffee table to help steady herself.)

GRACE. How do you know that? How do you know God?

GUY. People who end their lives think they know more than God.

GRACE. No, I don't. I don't think I know more than God. In fact, I *know* I don't because I have no earthly clue why he would create such a world – a world like this.

(In her sorrow, GRACE lets gun droop.)

GUY. Only God can give and take a life.

(He tries to grab the gun from GRACE. Lifting the gun back up, she holds it steady on GUY. once more, continuing to press her point.)

GRACE. Listen, I am one, tiny little puzzle piece in this world. I don't pretend to know all the pieces but I know mine. My piece. And if I was meant to "be" then I wouldn't be able to do it, right? To end it? That's what I figure. I mean, if by God, we were not allowed to take our own life, then it would be impossible for me to do so. Am I right?

(Testing God, GRACE puts the gun to her temple and begins to squeeze the trigger. GUY leaps for the gun, knocks it out of GRACE's hand, then grabs the phone. He is trembling, but anchored in his new found boldness.)

GUY. *(dialing the phone, 9-1-1)* Yes. That's right, Grace.

You are so right. You wouldn't be able to do it. *(into phone)* Yes, I have a girl here who's taken some sleeping pills. You'd never know it by how much she talks but... *(looking at airline tickets)* Yes, that's the address – six thirty-six, North Orange Drive. *(beat)* I think some time before three-thirty this morning, but not too much time before then. *(beat)* Uh... She's been going in and out, yes. *(interrupting abruptly)* Listen, are you coming or not?! One minute away? How do they get here so fast? *(beat)* Who? Who sent it? *(A smile grows in hope.)* Well, that was very observant of him. You tell that Brian, "Thank you."

*(**GUY** puts hand over phone, to **GRACE**.)*

See, Grace? He must have "seen" you, even over the phone – Brian, the guy at the alarm place. Brian sent the ambulance to help you. *(back into phone)* Who me? Oh, I'm just a friend. Her friend.

GRACE. *(with hope)* My friend?

GUY. Yes.

*(**GRACE** starts to cry.)*

GUY. *(into phone)* Well, I don't know why, really. *(making something up)* We were uh...planning a trip to Niagara Falls and I came home and the airline had sent us tickets to Cabo San Lucas by mistake.

GRACE. *(the high-pitched moan)* Uhhhhh.

GUY. *(whispering to **GRACE**)* Sorry.

(back into phone)

Just one mistake after another. We all experience them I suppose, but when a few come in a row, well I guess it can get a little overwhelming. *(beat)* Yes, I'll take care of it. *(correcting himself)* Her. I'll take care of *her*. *(beat)* Well, I'm going to simply exchange the tickets.

(He picks up tickets from coffee table and checks to see if they're exchangeable.)

Yes. That's what I'm going to do. I'm sure they'll

exchange them and when this mess is over and my girl, Grace, is feeling better, I might just take her on a nice, peaceful trip to Niagara Falls.

*(With one arm, **GRACE** reaches out for **GUY**. He takes her hand. There are sounds of an ambulance drawing near.)*

Is there anything I can do while we wait, coffee? Anything? *(beat)* Oh, okay – "just hold her." Fine. I can do that. But not like the photo near the fake waterfall. *(beat)* Oh, nothing operator. It's an inside joke. Hold on a second, please.

*(**GUY** sets the phone down and cradles **GRACE** in his arms. He then picks the phone back up.)*

Okay. Got her. We're fine now, operator. *(listening to the ambulance pulling into driveway)* They're here! Yes, that's them. Thank you very, very much.

*(He hangs up the phone and continues to cradle **GRACE**. in his arms, gently stroking her face.)*

They're here, Grace. They're here. And everything's going to be fine now. Everything's going to be just fine.

(Lights fade)

End of Play

COSTUME PLOT

JACK. Black t-shirt with black jeans

GUY. Black, button-down shirt with long sleeves and black pants

GRACE. A floor-length, smooth flowing, soft nightgown

SOUND PLOT

House alarm (10:35 minutes)

Phone ringing (1:24 minutes)

Ambulance with ambulance door (1 minute)

FURNITURE AND PROPERTY PLOT

FURNITURE:

Large, tattered old couch
Coffee table
Two trunks
Small table
Large area rug

PERSONAL PROPS:

JACK.
Two cloth laundry sacks
Piece of rope
Gun
Large, black flashlight
Pair of panty hose
Car keys

GUY.

Small camping flashlight
Pair of panty hose
Watch

GRACE.

Homemade, knitted blanket

PRESET PROPS:
Alarm box (on wall DSR, near front door)
Two throw pillows (on couch)
Cordless telephone (under something SR)
Airline tickets in envelope (on coffee table)
Frame with photo of a couple by a waterfall (on table SR)
Framed photo or drawing of Niagara Falls (on 2nd trunk against SL wall)
Small key to trunk (hidden in arm of couch)
Various boxes with names written on them
Various items in boxes to be removed during play
Various items for Jack to stuff in his laundry sack (off USR)
Brochures to Cabo San Lucas (on coffee table)
White negligee (in box SR)
Car seat magnetic pad (on couch)
Silver in silver box (in large trunk DSL)
Sleeping pills jar (in bathroom, off left)
Whiskey jar (empty, in bathroom, off left)
Two glasses of water (in bathroom)
Jar of aspirin (in bathroom)
Box of tissue (on trunk DSL)
Bowl of ice and water (off USR)
Wash cloth (off USR)
Light switch (on SL wall)

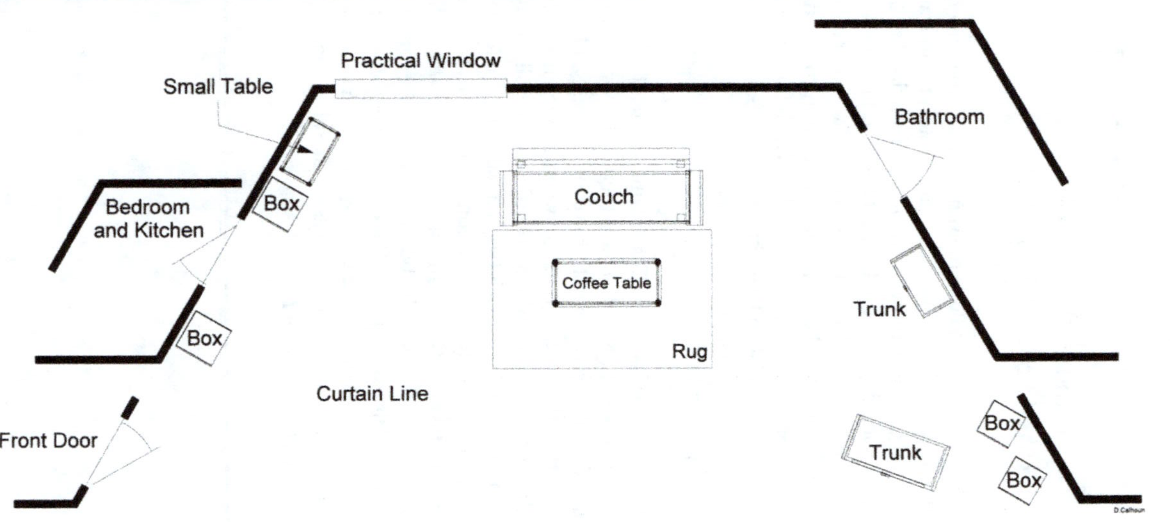

Scene Design
"CABO SAN LUCAS"

www.ingramcontent.com/pod-product-compliance
Lightning Source LLC
Chambersburg PA
CBHW070420120726
47909CB00005B/1727